W9-BNW-339

A QUIET PLACE

A QUIET PLACE

BY

Douglas Wood

ILLUSTRATED BY

Dan Andreasen

ALADDIN PAPERBACKS
New York London Toronto Sydney

ALADDIN PAPERBACKS

An imprint of Simon & Schuster Children's Publishing Division

1230 Avenue of the Americas, New York, NY 10020

Text copyright © 2002 by Douglas Wood

Illustrations copyright © 2002 by Dan Andreasen

All rights reserved, including the right of reproduction in whole or in part in any form.

ALADDIN PAPERBACKS and colophon are trademarks of Simon & Schuster, Inc.

Also available in a Simon & Schuster Books for Young Readers hardcover edition.

Designed by Paul Zakris

The text of this book was set in Diotima Roman.

Manufactured in China

First Aladdin Paperbacks edition May 2005

2 4 6 8 10 9 7 5 3

The Library of Congress has cataloged the hardcover edition as follows:

Wood, Douglas, 1951–

A quiet place / by Douglas Wood; illustrated by Dan Andreasen

p. cm.

Summary: Text and illustrations describe some of the special places that one can go to
be quiet and alone and to imagine, such as the woods, a seashore, a library, or inside oneself.

ISBN 0-689-81511-5 (hc.)

[1. Solitude—Fiction. 2. Imagination—Fiction.] I. Andreasen, Dan; ill. II. Title.

PZ7.W84738Qu   2001

[E]—dc21   98-38102

CIP

ISBN 0-689-87609-2 (pbk.)

To all who listen . . .
—D. W.

To Bret
—D. A.

Sometimes a person needs a quiet place.

A place to rest your ears from
     bells ringing and
     whistles shrieking and
     grown-ups talking and
     engines roaring and
     horns blaring and
     grown-ups talking and
     radios playing and
     grown-ups . . .
     Well, even grown-ups need a quiet place sometimes.

But it can be hard to find one.
You have to know where to look.

You could look under a bush,
    a lilac bush, in your own backyard.
    When you crawl underneath it,
    all the sounds of the world seem
    soft and far away.
    And you can be a pirate
    finding buried treasure
    on a desert island.
    A bush could be your quiet place.

Until someone calls you to clean your room. Then . . .

You could look in the woods.
    You might find an old stump for a chair
    or a mossy log for a couch
    in a green mansion of shadows and sunbeams.
    It's not really quiet, of course.
    Blue jays scream warnings, and wind sings in the leaves.
    But it *feels* quiet. And you can be a timber wolf,
    the gray ghost of the forest.
    The woods could be your quiet place.

But if the woods are too dark and deep . . .

You could look by the sea
　　on a beach in the early morning fog.
　　Your footprints are the first of the day.
　　The waves are roaring,
　　and the gulls are crying,
　　but it doesn't seem noisy.
　　And you can just be an explorer
　　discovering a lost continent.
　　The beach could be your quiet place.

But if the beach is not your cup of tea . . .

You could look in the desert,
     where Old Man Saguaro reaches for the sky,
     and far-off thunderheads bloom
     like sky-flowers over the mesas.
     A cactus wren drops by for a visit,
     while a horned toad blinks in the sun.
     And you can be a Pony Express rider
     galloping through the Old West.
     The desert could be your quiet place.

But if the desert is a bit too dry . . .

You could sit by a pond.
    A heron by the shore
    stands still as a tree branch,
    and the water is so calm it looks like a mirror.
    Then a frog plops from a lily pad,
    and your face begins to wiggle.
    And you can be the world's greatest fisherman
    reeling in a monster catch.
    A pond could be your quiet place.

But if the fish aren't biting . . .

You could look in a cavern
        where every footstep echoes,
        and the slow *drip, drip* of water
        builds new rocks that hang like icicles
        or stand like sculptures;
        where days and nights and weeks and years
        are all the same.
        And you can be a cave dweller
        in the lair of the saber-toothed tiger.
        A cave could be your quiet place.

But if a cave is too cold and damp . . .

You could climb to the top of a hill
  where clouds float by like ships
  or alligators or elephants.
  On a hilltop you can see a long way
  and think long thoughts
  about How and What and Why.
  And you can be a mountain climber
  on the top of the world.
  A hilltop could be your quiet place.

But if your legs are too tired for climbing . . .

You could wait for a snowy day
and lie down in a snowdrift.
All around you the falling snow whispers, "S-H-H-H-H,"
and wraps the world in silence.
If you listen closely, you can almost hear it breathing.
You breathe softly, too, pretending to be
a polar bear sleeping
in a land where the snowy silence never ends.
A snowdrift could be your quiet place.

But if it's too warm for snowdrifts . . .

You could visit a museum
    where brass tigers and bronze lions
    stand silent guard over fabulous treasures.
    Every painting is a magic window
    that your own imagination
    can open wide and climb through.
    And you can be an artist
    admiring your own masterpiece.
    A museum could be your quiet place.

But if the museum is closed for renovation . . .

You could go to a secret corner of the library
    where the only people talking
    are between the covers of books.
    They speak so softly
    you can only hear them in your head
    as you read about forests and oceans and deserts
    and caverns and museums
    and a thousand other things.
    A library could be your quiet place.

But if the library isn't open yet . . .

You could come home
    and clean your room
    and read your own books
    and think your own thoughts
    and feel your own feelings
    and discover the very best quiet place of all—
    the one that's always there, no matter
    where you go or where you stay—

the one inside of you.